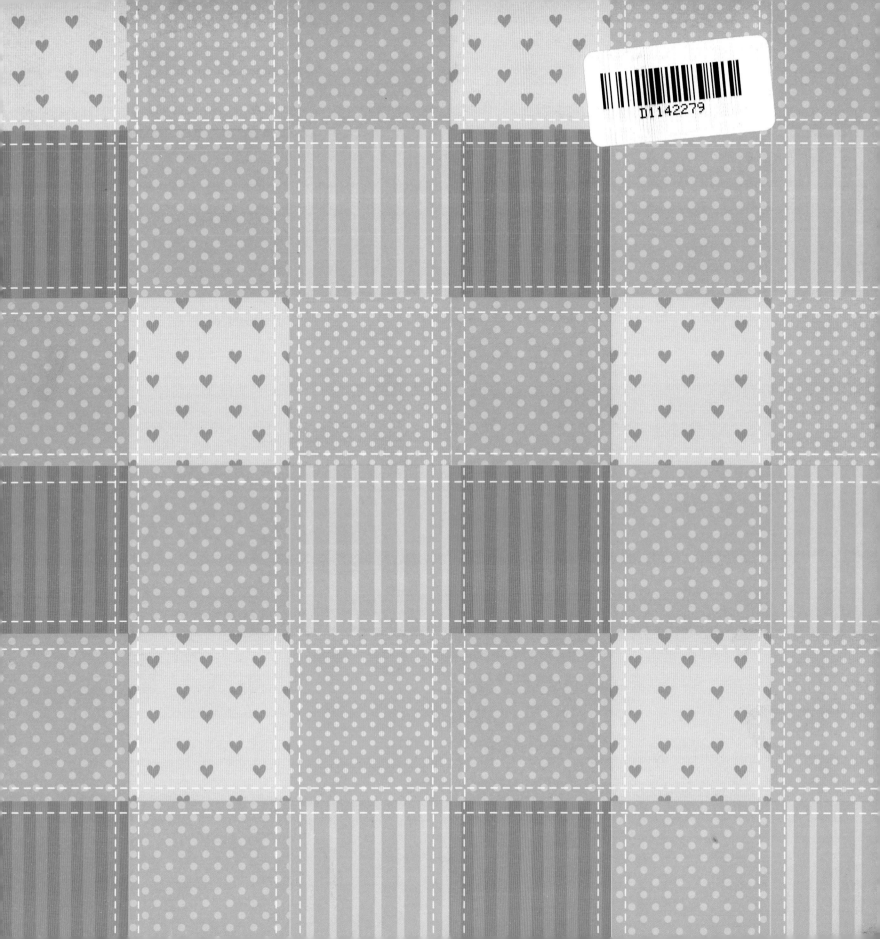

For Ruby, the original and best Honey bunny x - C.S.
For Chloe and Owen - S.W.

This edition first published in 2013 by Alligator Books Ltd.
Cupcake is an imprint of Alligator Books Ltd
Gadd House, Arcadia Avenue, London N3 2JU, UK

www.alligatorbooks.co.uk

Written by Christine Swift
Illustrated by Sarah Wade

Printed in China.   11423

I love you Honey Bunny

Written by
Christine Swift

Illustrated by
Sarah Wade

cupcake

The skies darkened above, raindrops started to fall.
Honey bunny suddenly felt very small.

"Quick, Honey bunny, the skies have turned black.
I don't want to get wet, we must *hurry* back."

"Hold my hand tight mummy,
if you could.
I don't want to get lost
as we run through the woods."

They ran through the woods,
as the rain tumbled down.
Scared forest creatures
ran all around.

Fast into the burrow, out of the rain.

Honey bunny and mummy were safe again.

Inside it was cosy,
the fire kept them warm.

Honey bunny and mummy
were out of the storm.

A loud clap of thunder echoed through the skies.

Poor Honey bunny had tears in her eyes.

"I'm scared of the thunder!

Mummy hold me tight.
When you hold me, I know that I'll be alright."

They snuggled under a blanket,
to talk about their day.

"I love you Honey bunny",
"Always". said mummy.

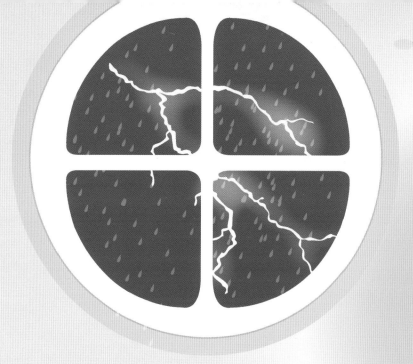

"Mummy,

I love YOU,

you're such a great mum."

"You make me feel special,
you make everything fun."

"When I am lonely, when I want to play."

"You come along to brighten my day."

"When I hurt my hand, it made me cry."

"You gave me a plaster
and wiped the tears from my eyes."

"When I try my hardest,
    when I'm put to the test."

"You make me feel proud
because I did my best."

"Oh Honey bunny,

you make **me**
feel so proud!"

Mummy span Honey bunny, up and around.

"Look, the sun's shining,
the rain's gone away.
Honey bunny, it's time
to go outside and play."

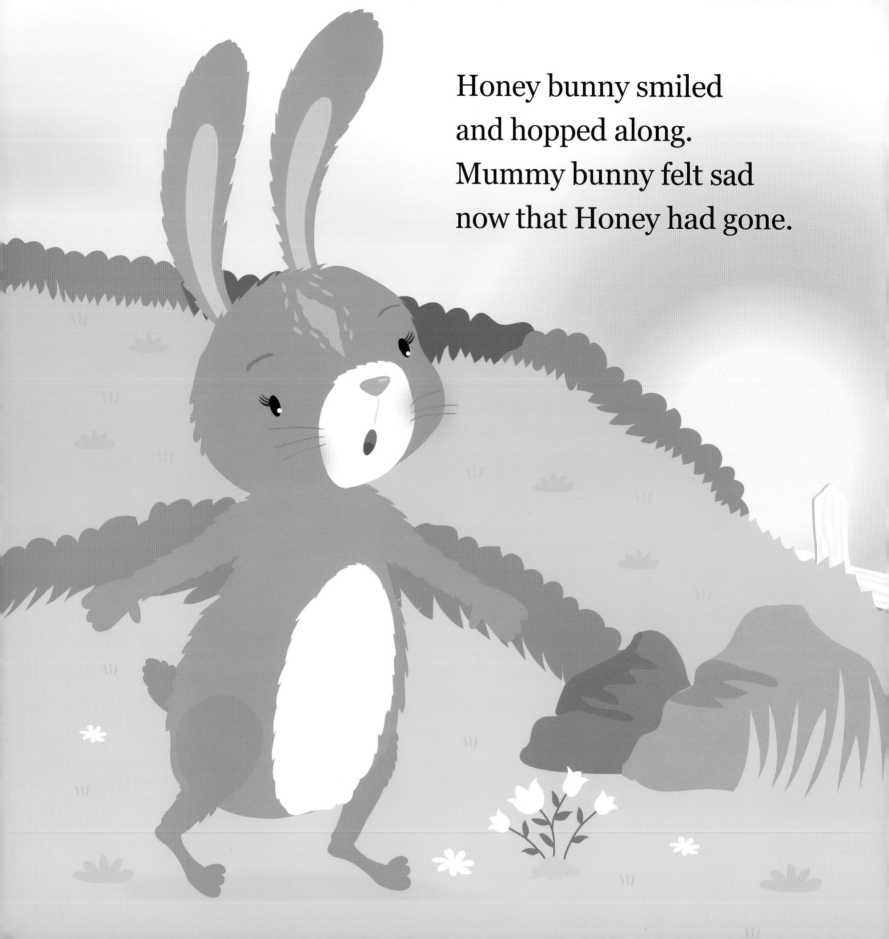

Honey bunny smiled
and hopped along.
Mummy bunny felt sad
now that Honey had gone.

"Wait for me, Honey bunny,
I'm coming too."

"I have so much fun
when I play with you."

They played hide and seek,

they played bunny jump high.

They played hunt the acorn,

they counted clouds in the sky.

The stars started twinkling,

the moon shone overhead.

"Another fun day tomorrow, Honey bunny,"
mummy said.

Night, night.

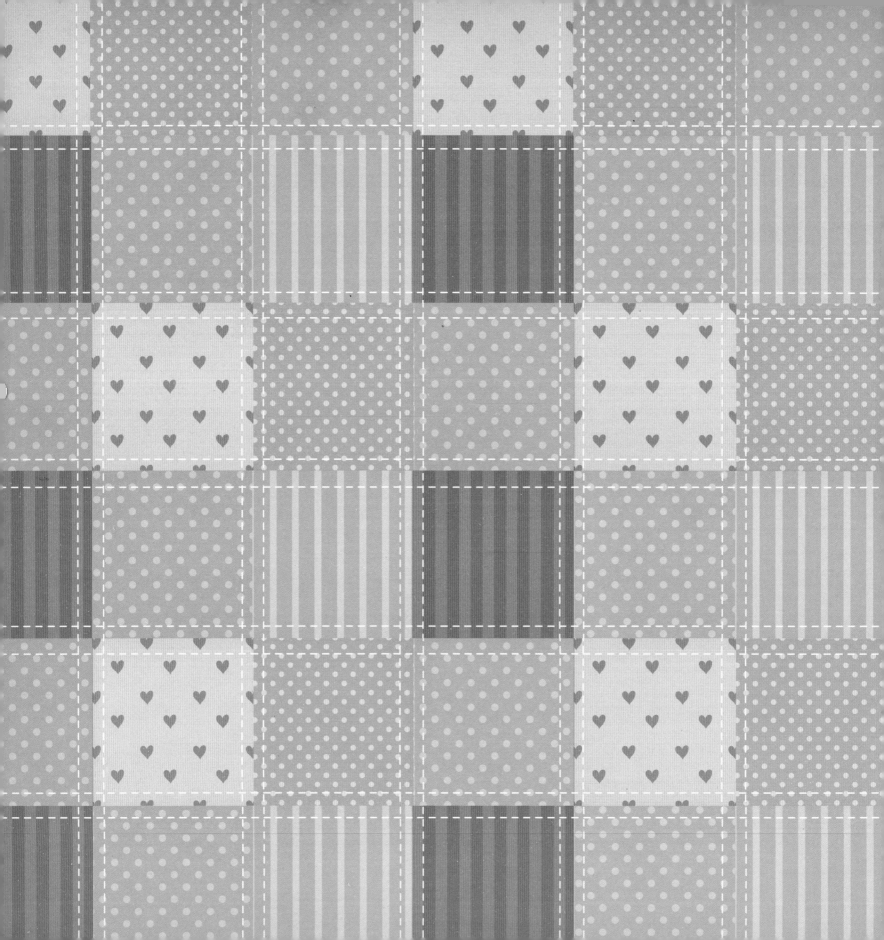